The Lion
and the
Gypsy

by Jillian Powell
and Heather Deen

Evans

First published 2009
Evans Brothers Limited
2A Portman Mansions
Chiltern St
London W1U 6NR

Text copyright © Jillian Powell 2009
© in the illustrations Evans Brothers Ltd 2009

British Library Cataloguing in Publication Data

Powell, Jillian.
   The lion and the gypsy – (Skylarks)
   1. Children's stories.
   I. Title II. Series
   823.9'14-dc22

ISBN-13: HB 978 0 237 53905 4
ISBN-13: PB 978 0 237 53892 7

Printed in China by New Era Printing Co. Ltd

Series Editor: Louise John
Design: Robert Walster
Production: Jenny Mulvanny

Contents

Chapter One

At night, the desert stirs. The stars wink in a velvet sky. The moon is high. A scorpion scurries across the sand as it cools from the heat of the day. Jerboas bounce like tiny kangaroos in search of plants and seeds to eat. A fox moves briskly in the light of the moon.

And a sand-coloured lion comes down from the sand hills. In the day, the desert is still and smells of nothing but heat. But now the lion sniffs the air for tasty morsels to eat. For a moment, he stands still as a rock for he can smell the scent of a human.

The sand lies rippled like folded silk. The lion's feet sink into it as he pads silently across the desert. He has seen footprints in the distance. The moon is filling them with violet shadows. Silently, he moves closer. But these are no ordinary footprints. This is some strange three-legged animal. For each step he counts three clear prints, one, two, three. The lion is curious and a little afraid. But the scent of a human is still in the air. He follows the footprints, his ears pricked, his eyes glinting.

Chapter Two

Down by the river, Fatima was feeling
tired. She had been rowing her little
boat up and down the slow-running
river between the sand hills of the
desert. Fatima was a wandering gypsy
who sang for her living. Every day, she
travelled from place to place, finding

her way by the moon and the stars.
She carried only three things with her:
her mandolin, her water jar and a stout
wooden stick for walking. But now
Fatima's bare feet were tired from
walking over the sun-baked sand.

At each step, her walking stick sank more heavily into the sand. She had earned just a few silver coins in return for her songs, which she carried in a purse hidden under her striped robes.

At last, Fatima put down her few belongings and lay on the sand to rest. The sun had sunk behind the hills. The moon was shining brightly. It cast its silvery light on the river and sent dark shadows creeping between the sand dunes. Fatima soon fell fast asleep. She kept her stout walking stick in her hand, and her water jar and mandolin close beside her. As she slept, Fatima began to dream. She dreamed she was in a beautiful garden shaded by palm trees, where the sound of her mandolin filled the air. Coconuts and dates hung from

the trees and a babbling fountain was
cooling the air. People were gathered
around, smiling at the music.
They threw coins into the fountain
in thanks.

Fatima slept so soundly she did not hear the sand-coloured lion padding across the sand towards her. His long mane rippled. His tail stood upright. His golden eyes glistened in the moonlight. He crept closer. Here, where the mysterious three-legged footprints tailed off, was the human sleeping on the sand, and she smelt good enough to eat.

On silent paws he crept around her, sniffing hungrily. Round and round he circled. Where should he begin? This was a good meal indeed. All the time, Fatima lay sound asleep, lost in her dream. She had no idea of the danger she was in.

Chapter Three

As she slept, Fatima still held the
walking stick in her hand. The lion saw
this and he crept closer. He thought
he could grab Fatima's arm and the
walking stick with it. His strong jaws
opened wide. But as he crouched over
her, his long mane tickled Fatima's face.

In her dream, the water of the fountain began to splash and tickle her face. Still sleeping, she hit out with her stick as she did when the midges were biting. The lion sprang back, startled. Still the gypsy was fast asleep. He waited for a while. Then he saw Fatima's water jar, and he thought he might

have a drink before eating her. The
water in the jar would be cool and fresh,
not warm like the water in the river.

The lion crept slowly and silently towards the jar. He didn't want to wake her. But there was something in the jar besides the water! A white face was staring up at him! It was the moon. The moon was staring up at him from the water jar! It seemed to be smiling and winking at him.

He jumped back in alarm. His tail swished angrily. There was something magical about this gypsy who kept the moon in a water jar! He had better eat her up quickly, before she put a spell on him. Perhaps the mandolin by her side contained magic powers that would protect her.

Chapter Four

The lion waited a while to make sure
that the gypsy was still sleeping. Then
he crept closer, sniffing hungrily. He
crouched over the mandolin, his nose
twitching. But he got too close and
the strings caught his nose. Twang!

The lion reeled backwards and the

noise of the mandolin woke Fatima. She opened her eyes and looked around her. Then she saw the lion crouching close

by her. His tail was swishing from side to side, making rivers in the sand.

Slowly, quietly, Fatima sat up. Slowly, quietly, she crossed her legs. Slowly, quietly, she picked up her mandolin and began to play. As she played, Fatima and the lion sat watching each other.

Fatima did not know the lion thought she had magic powers. She was afraid he was going to eat her, but she hoped her music might charm him. She had heard of people who could charm snakes. Why not a lion?

She sat very still, playing her mandolin. The song she played was soft and gentle. The music wafted across the desert. All the while, the lion sat a little way away, watching and waiting. The music had calmed his nerves but he was still hungry. He was waiting for his chance. But he was afraid the gypsy might cast a spell on him. After all, this woman who walked with three legs and played the mandolin so sweetly, had trapped the moon in her water jar.

Chapter Five

After some time, Fatima stopped playing. The lion was still there, watching and waiting. He looked as if he was about to pounce. She had seen cats crouch like this, as still as a statue, only the twitch of a tail betraying their intent. If she could not charm him with her music, perhaps she could bribe him with coins. She reached for her purse and sprinkled the coins on the sand. They lay shining like little moons and the lion stood transfixed. First the moon in a jar and now moon money?

Fatima nodded to the lion, as if to say the coins are yours. But money could not buy this lion. Money was no good for hunger. He pawed at the sand impatiently. Fatima panicked. If she could not charm him or bribe him, there was nothing else for it. She must fight him off with her walking stick.

She reached out for the stick but her hand trembled. The lion saw her tremble and began to wonder if she was a magical gypsy after all. He threw back his head and snarled. His teeth flashed like daggers. No stick was a match for this animal.

Fatima's mind was racing. She had only one thing left to try. She had cool fresh water in her water jar. She grabbed hold of the jar and held it out to the lion.

"Drink, lion. The water is cold and refreshing!" she told him.

But the lion was having none of this trickery.

"Gypsy, you cannot trick me with the moon water!" he roared. He shook his mane and prepared to pounce.

Chapter Six

Fatima's heart was pounding. Her mouth was dry. She gulped at the cold water then hurled the empty jar at the lion. The water jar rolled at his feet. The last drops sank into the thirsty sand. The lion peered inside curiously. But the moon had gone!

Now he knew that this gypsy had magic powers. She had drunk the moon! He pawed at the jar, rolling it over and over in the sand. Then he saw that the gypsy was watching him with bright round eyes. He decided he must eat her at once, before she magicked him into the water jar!

He gave a huge roar and pounced.
But Fatima, realising that the lion
had been fooled by the moon's reflection
in the water jar, leaped aside.

She snatched up the jar and held it
in front of her.

"Lion!" she said in a commanding voice. "You saw me magic the moon away. Now I can do the same to you! Follow my music and I will show you where I have put the moon!"

Holding her stick and her water jar beneath her arm, Fatima picked up her mandolin and began to play.

Puzzled, the lion followed her.

The gypsy led him across the soft rippled sand to the river. The lion was still wary but he crept closer, hoping to catch the gypsy from behind. But as they reached the river, Fatima stopped playing. She turned round and held up her wooden stick like a magic wand.

"Now you are invisible!" she told the lion. "For look, there you are with the moon!"

Chapter Seven

The lion crept down to the river. He peered into it. The gypsy was right! There he was, trapped in the river with the moon right beside him. Witchery! He let out a roar and the lion in the river did the same. He could see his long mane rippling, his tail swishing.

Witchery!

"Now, if you do as I say, I can magic you back from the river!" the gypsy told him. "But to break this spell, first I must catch the moon."

The lion stood amazed as Fatima climbed into her little boat. She laid her stick, her mandolin and her water jar beside her.

Slowly, she began to row towards the image of the moon, which shone plump and white in the middle of the river. The lion followed the boat along the bank. This gypsy was indeed a witch. She must catch the moon and release him from this watery spell.

"There!" he roared, running along the bank. "There it is!" he pointed with the tip of his nose.

"Where?" asked Fatima, rowing a little further.

"There, there!" the lion roared. But as he ran along the bank, the moon seemed to run with him. First it was here, and then it was there. The lion was getting tired, and still the gypsy had not caught the moon. Her oars made the water dance, and the moon wobbled and vanished as if it was playing hide and seek.

38

Chapter Eight

All the while, Fatima kept rowing slowly
and surely across the river. At last, she
reached the other side. She climbed out
of her boat, picked up her mandolin and
her water jar, and took her stick in her
hand. The lion roared angrily from the
other side of the river.

"Wait!" he roared. "One, the moon is still in the river. Two, I am still in the river and three, I am still hungry!"

Fatima finished tying her boat up. She looked across at the lion.

"Wait by the river bank until daybreak," she called. "My magic will not work until dawn. Then the moon will return to the sky where it belongs, and you will return to the sand hills where you belong. But as for the third thing…" she told the lion. "I am afraid I cannot help you there, Lion!"

And with that, Fatima turned and walked across the sand hills and away to safety.

41

End note

This story was inspired by a famous painting called 'The Sleeping Gypsy' by the French artist, Henri Rousseau (1844 – 1910). The painting, which dates from 1897, is in the Museum of Modern Art in New York.

Rousseau described the painting in a letter:

"A wandering Negress, a mandolin player, lies with her jar beside her (a vase with drinking water), overcome by fatigue in a deep sleep. A lion chances to pass by, picks up her scent yet does not devour her. There is a moonlight effect, very poetic. The scene is set in a completely arid desert. The gypsy is dressed in oriental costume."

If you enjoyed this story, why not read another *Skylarks* book?

Josie's Garden
by David Orme and Martin Remphry

Josie lives in a high-rise flat in town with her mum and brother. More than anything else in the world, Josie wants a garden. When Josie and her friend, Meena, discover an abandoned and over-grown garden near their school, Josie is delighted and decides to make the garden her own. But sometimes, things are not quite as simple as they first seem...

The Emperor's New Clothes

by Louise John and Serena Curmi

There once lived an emperor who was proud and vain and spent all his money on clothes. One day, two scoundrels arrived at the palace and persuaded the emperor that they could weave magical cloth. He set them to work making him a fine set of robes.

But the emperor had a lesson to learn, and his new clothes were quite a sight to behold!

Carving the Sea Path

by Kathryn White and Evelyn Duverne

When Samuel first moves to the Arctic, he is rude and unfriendly. But Irniq gives him a chance, and the boys become friends. Then, as the summer comes to an end, the boys quarrel and drift apart. One day, Irniq finds a trapped whale under the ice, and doesn't know what to do. Luckily, Samuel appears and knows exactly who can help. Will the boys save the whale in time?

Noah's Shark
by Alan Durant and Holly Surplice

Noah was fed up with the people in his world making a right mess of everything. He built a big boat to escape in, and invited his animal friends along – couples only! The animals queued up by the boat, two by two. All except for Mrs Shark, who came alone. It seemed she had accidentally eaten her husband! Would Noah be able to trust her on his boat?

Skylarks titles include:

Awkward Annie
by Julia Williams and Tim Archbold
HB 9780237533847 / PB 9780237534028

Sleeping Beauty
by Louise John and Natascia Ugliano
HB 9780237533861 / PB 9780237534042

Detective Derek
by Karen Wallace and Beccy Blake
HB 9780237533885 / PB 9780237534066

Hurricane Season
by David Orme and Doreen Lang
HB 9780237533892 / PB 9780237534073

Spiggy Red
by Penny Dolan and Cinzia Battistel
HB 9780237533854 / PB 9780237534035

London's Burning
by Pauline Francis and Alessandro Baldanzi
HB 9780237533878 / PB 9780237534059

The Black Knight
by Mick Gowar and Graham Howells
HB 9780237535803 / PB 9780237535926

Ghost Mouse
by Karen Wallace and Beccy Blake
HB 9780237535827 / PB 9780237535940

Yasmin's Parcels
by Jill Atkins and Lauren Tobia
HB 9780237535858 / PB 9780237535971

Muffin
by Anne Rooney and Sean Julian
HB 9780237535810 / PB 9780237535933

Tallulah and the Tea Leaves
by Louise John and Vian Oelofsen
HB 9780237535841 / PB 9780237535964

The Big Purple Wonderbook
by Enid Richemont and Helen Jackson
HB 9780237535834 / PB 9780237535957

Noah's Shark
by Alan Durant and Holly Surplice
HB 9780237539047 / PB 9780237538910

The Emperor's New Clothes
by Louise John and Serena Curmi
HB 9780237539085 / PB 9780237538958

Carving the Sea Path
by Kathryn White and Evelyn Duverne
HB 9780237539030 / PB 9780237538903

Merbaby
by Penny Kendal and Claudia Venturini
HB 9780237539078 / PB 9780237538941

The Lion and the Gypsy
by Jillian Powell and Heather Deen
HB 9780237539054 / PB 9780237538927

Josie's Garden
by David Orme and Martin Remphry
HB 9780237539061 / PB 9780237538934